Of Rhinos and Horns

Ron Mueller

Of Rhinos and Horns

Of Rhinos and Horns

Books and Stories by Ron Mueller

<u>**Fiction Series**</u>
The Alex Evercrest Series
The River Front
The Girl on The Grill
Missing
Maggot
Racist
Votive Candles
Windy City
Country Road
Pool of Blood
Sins of the Daughter
Body Parts
The Skull Collector
The Vanishing
The Shadow Fighter
Moonshine
Grief's Trajectory
The Magic Touch
Northern Lights
Alex Evercrest Heroine
Alex Evercrest Collection Two
New Direction
A Family Affair
Disruption
Aftermath
The St. Lebuinnus Church Murder

A Brian O'Neil Novel
Hawaiian Phoenix
Moon Curser
Death Broker

The Problem Solver Series
Solutions
Drug Lords
Border Crosser
The Problem Solver Collection

<u>**The Taelo Series**</u>
The Early Years
The Golden Feather
Journey of Discovery
Dangerous Passage
Condor Clan Slingers
Circumvention
The Journey of Sages
Collection
Future Leaders Journey

<u>**A Taelo Story:**</u>
White Swan and Quiet Pheasant
The Child's Name
Floating Cloud
Quiet Rabbit
Busy Bee
Little Otter & Talking Wren
Broken Spear
Burley Bear & Meadow Flower
Taelo Story Collection

<u>**Science Fiction**</u>

The Savitar Series:
Journey's End
Savitar
Confluence
Savitar Series Collection

Bram Nielson Series
The Fold
The Message
Fold Wormhole
Negative Fold
Ripples in Time
Bram Nielson Collection

<u>**Single Science Fiction Books:**</u>
Current Past and Future
The Event
The Door
Viajante 7

The Problem Solver Book 4

 *Of Rhinos and Horns*

Ron Mueller

Around the World Publishing LLC
Cincinnati, Ohio

This book is a work of fiction. Names, characters, places, and incidents either are products of the author's imagination or are used fictitiously. Any resemblance to actual events or locales or persons, living or dead, is entirely coincidental.

Of Rhinos and Horns ©

ISBN 13: 978-1-68223-976-6

Distributed by: Ingram
Cover Picture: by Bruce Rolff @Dreamstime
Cover Design: by Ron Mueller

<u>Dedication</u>

To the survival of the Rhino

Introduction

It is a troubled world. The human species has, like no other, risen to dominate the world. The rise is marked with amazing beauty and grace. It is also marked by cruelty to other humans and a disregard for the negative impact they have on their only home, the earth.

The beauty found in poetry and writing, the beauty found in paintings and sculptors is more than countered by the wars, the intentional environmental destruction, and the barriers each separate country imposes on its peoples and the neighboring states.

The belief of limited resources, the behavior of greed, the desire for wealth and the desire for control are all factors in the behavior exhibited by those who surface at the top of the heap. The ability of various leaders, in a myriad of areas, to convince those more interested in their immediate family well-being allows those interested in domination to rise to positions of influence and power.

Often their belief is that they have been ordained to be in charge or alternately they are smarter and should be in the lead.

The rise of the rule of law has created a situation where fairness is managed by laws developed by the representatives of the people. Even in the situation found in the United States that has three branches of government designed to maintain the system of fairness to all, slavery, and women's right to vote were initially missed. More recently the rights of gay or lesbian people are in question.

Human greed, cruelty, misbehavior, and disregard of the environment seems to increase asymptotically with the rapid rise of the population.

Justice is not always served. This situation is managed by a secret organization that funds and directs the actions of ***The Problem-solver***. This is a person whose principles, judgement, behavior, and actions guide him in how to resolve problems that otherwise would be left unchecked.

The problems are many. The problems are anywhere in the world. The problems are solved in the best manner that The Problem-solver determines.

See if you agree with the problem resolutions, that this Problem-solver, ***Ian Sinclair***, has chosen for his various assignments.

<u>*Of Rhinos and Horns*</u>

<u>*1 Lazy Lady*</u>

*T*heir escape from the pirates was the most dramatic event in Maurice's and Ted's lives. Matt's handling of the battle was a lesson in preparation and in how to totally devastate your opponent. Only a few of the twenty some attack pirate boats disappeared in what seemed to be a crater created by the explosion of every boat.

Then the command ship attacked and once again it seemed that they were going to be captured by a ship armed with a deck cannon that put a shell on each side of the Lazy Lady.

Then Maurice watched as Matt pressed a button and the entire front end of the giant on coming ship blew up as if it had been hit by some unseen rocket.

She rejoiced when Matt asked Ted to hoist the main sail and the jib, and she felt the Lazy Lady come to life and seemingly leap forward in joy.

They sailed into Cape Town where Matt left them.

A short time after they docked Matt left them to return to the US.

She and Ted sailed the Lazy Lady out of Cape Town to continue on their around the world sailing tour. They sailed north along the coast of Africa. They stopped at almost every port for a day so that they could enjoy the various historic sites but mostly because it allowed them to enjoy the wide variety of dishes and did not have to cook or clean. This took them several months and then before entering the Med, they returned to the US to celebrate the births of grandchildren and spend a few days with the new children.

They were known to the family as the grandparents that sailed the world. Maurice accepted the title with pride and offered to pay the airfare for any family member that desired to join them on the Lazy Lady.

After being away for more than a month they returned to the Lazy Lady that they had come to considered home. Each time they returned they would talk about the time they were saved by Matt from being taken hostage by the Pirates of the coast of East Africa. They would laugh at the fact that they had never asked and now did not know his last name. They would have loved dearly to communicate with him and share the highlights of their journey.

They sailed into the Mediterranean and did a counter clockwise tour. They stopped in Algiers, Tunis, Tripoli and when four months later they got to Alexandria, they once again flew back to the US to celebrate Thanksgiving.

After enjoying the family and all their grandchildren they decided to stay for Christmas. This allowed them to play Santa parents and spoil their brewed of grandchildren.

On their return they continued on and went to see Jerusalem where they spent more than a week visiting all the religious sites.

They then sailed to Beirut and from there sailed to Cyprus. They stopped briefly in Antalya, Turkey to rejuvenate and get the Lazy Lady refreshed.

Then it was on to Athens where they spent a week visiting all the historic sites that they had studied in high school and college.

Then up northward up eastern side of the Adriatic Sea with brief stops in several of sea ports. The longest stay was at the very northern part when they reached Venice. They toured Venice for a week and then sailed nonstop to Catania, Sicily before going on to Naples.

There they once again left the Lazy Lady while they flew home for several grandchildren's graduations from high school and college. This was only a brief visit, and, on their return, they sailed to Fiumicino where they anchored for a week as they visited Rome. Their next stop was Livorno where they stopped so they could take a road trip to Florence.

The sailing continue for the rest of the year as the two visited Genoa, Nice, Marseille Barcelona and Valencia.

They left the Mediterranean and sailed north and stopped in Lisbon.

From there they sailed straight to Dublin where they stayed for more than a month to tour Ireland. It was during this period that they once again flew back to the states.

They continued their sailing for yet two more years and would spend time visiting many of the cities in the UK, spent a month in Amsterdam and then took a boat tour down the Rhine to Switzerland and back.

They chuckled when they lined the Lazy Lady with a row of potted flowers.

They waited until summer to sail into the Bering Sea and hit many of the ports like Helsinki, Stockholm and Copenhagen.

Their last stop on the way back to the States was Edinburgh where they spent several weeks relaxing and touring the countryside.

Once they made New York they took another family break and flew back to LA to celebrate in Pasadena where the majority of the family now lived.

After a few weeks they flew back to the Lazy lady.

Once they returned to the Lazy Lady, it took them another five years to bring her through the Panama canal and up the coast of Baja California. They finally docked the Lazy Lady and arranged for her complete overhaul.

The Lazy Lady was taken out of the water and literally refurbished and restored to the point where she was once again like new. Her engine and the appliance were all replaced.

They then sailed on her for almost another ten years and then when they could no longer do so on their own. They arranged to once again refurbish the Lazy Lady.

It was during this last time of renewing the Lazy Lady that after checking with their sons, they decided that the person who had rescued them from the pirates off the coast of Africa should be the new owner of the yacht that he had saved from the pirates.

Maurice had looked ahead and every year for the last five years she had held a family goodbye party. She had done much of the baking and preparation for the first party but for the other four years had the party catered. These parties let everyone involved deal with the fact that there was an end point to everyone's journey.

Shortly after, both went into Hospice care where they shared the same apartment for what they knew would be their final journey together. They had settled all their accounts and knew that they had shared a wonderous life together.

Their two sons who were now nearing their own retirement and their children who were now all grown adults themselves and who had children all stopped by to say their goodbyes.

Their wealth was significant but not exceedingly huge, most of their estate was in the business that they had passed on to their sons. However, there was still a sizeable amount that was in trust with specific instructions of how that was to be handled.

The biggest challenge that they had worked through was how to pass the Lazy Lady on to the one person who they agreed should be the one to inherit it.

They only knew him as Matt, so they put an advertisement in the personal section of several newspapers in major cities across the US that simply gave their names and the fact that they had been saved from being captured by pirates by someone sent to save them. They wanted to reward that person and needed to get in contact with him to make sure he accepted the ownership of the Lazy Lady.

They kept that Ad active for more than three years and were giving up hope when they received the call that they had waited for what to them seemed to be an eternity. They learned the name of the person they would pass the Lazy Lady to. It was less than a year later that they both took that name with them to eternity when within a month of each other they passed away.

The person who had contacted them was Ian's handler. He had met with Maurice's and Ted's lawyer and had made all the legal arrangements for the transfer. Not a month later he was online with Ian letting him know of their passing and the fact that they had left him the Lazy Lady as a measure of their gratitude.

The contact with Ian had more to do with a problem requiring his special touch than about the yacht. It had to do with a high stakes kidnapping that needed to be resolved. It needed the special touch of the Problem-Solver.

Ian knew immediately that he would put the Lazy Lady to work as part of the solution that he had in mind.

2 Rise to Power

General Ingraditi was frustrated by the situation of the current Army Command. He controlled much of the country, but his two longtime nemesis seemed to currently have the upper hand. For years he had been hounded by General Mumbada and his longtime friend General Wesbow who controlled about forty percent of the country. The two were inseparable and were able to fend off his many attempts to derail them and take complete control of the army.

He was upset with the support they were given by a group of wealthy businessmen that had great influence with the general assembly. It was a delicate situation that he knew he would win in the near future when it came to head that very likely might be a bloody confrontation.

He had the loyalty of the larger part of the army but that only meant that he could defend the territory he currently controlled and keep his adversaries at bay.

He knew that the richest part of Nairobi was in the hands of General Mumbada and the part of the army that had his loyalty. As long as that was the case, he would have to put up with General Mumbada.

As General Ingraditi lamented, needing to put up with his adversary, General Mumbada, followed by his longtime friend, Vice General Wesbow walked slowly down the line of soldiers they were inspecting.

The last two soldiers were dressed in very expensive black suites that had been awarded to them for their superior service to the army. The general lightly brushed the thousand-dollar suits and congratulated each of the soldiers for their superior service and shook their hands. He was sure that his reward-based recognition was loved by his army. He knew that they were loyal to him more than the parts of the army controlled by his superior.

He and General Wesbow were friends since their childhood when they were in grade school. At that time Kenya was still in the control of Great Briton and was known as British East Africa. The two of them were disturbed to see the British and European farmers prospering by growing coffee and tea on the rich Kenyan land while the general population was struggling to make ends meet. The two came to despise the inequity of the situation and throughout their younger years they and their friends played games where they rid the country of foreigners and became the leaders who took Kenya to higher power in the world.

He and Lionel Wesbow remained friends as they grew older. They had parents that pushed them to do well in school and later to get into the Army. The two went to and graduated from a school similar to the US army's West Point Academy.

He had the framed degree stating that Maurice Mumbada had graduated first in the class of 1976 proudly displayed on the wall of his office. He knew that Lionel had a similar degree that stated he had graduated second that he had hung in his office.

It was a time where the country's many clans and forty some differing languages kept the various clans apart from each other. In 1963 after facing internal rebellion, the British relinquished control and the following year Kenya became an independent nation.

Kiswahili became the common language. That was the language that the two had grown up with. They were fluent in English which put them in a great position as they made their way up the army ranks.

In the following years they focused on what it took to get ahead and made sure that both were at the right place at the right time. They were both rewarded with the promotions that they sought.

There was always the one person to whom they were both junior to and who seemed to be promoted just ahead of the two of them.

The two now in controlled of most of the western part of the country and wide strip that extended down to the Indian Ocean.

General Ingraditi, who they supposedly reported to controlled the eastern and northern part of Kenya.

Their reporting relationship with Ingraditi was frosty but they made sure that it would not reach the point of direct confrontation.

The area they controlled included Nairobi that was several million people strong and the entire area they controlled included sixty percent of the population.

They recognized that their main strength was the support of a group of wealthy businessmen that were prospering by having them look the other way to their across the border self-serving business dealings.

General Ingraditi controlled more territory and had to interface with four boundary countries whereas he only dealt with the politics of dealing with two border countries.

They felt certain that they had enough power that they could take control of the entire country, but it would put them at risk of a battle between the men loyal to them and those loyal to General Ingraditi. It would entail an internal battle that would not be good for them or the country. It was clear to them that it might increase their ability to add to the billions to what they already had in their Swiss bank accounts.

They decided they were in a strong position and should continue to wait to make their upward move when the opportunity presented itself.

General Ingraditi gave them the idea of how to increase the cash flow to their bank accounts. He periodically kidnapped some important business man and then demanded a ransom. When the ransom was paid the business man was released. The timing of the kidnappings varied but they were far enough apart that the public attention span waned, and another kidnapping did not alarm the population.

They liked that idea, but they planned to do the same on a grander scale. The opportunity to do so presented itself a few weeks after they had agreed to the ransom idea.

The Society of Geographic Exploration contacted General Mumbada and asked for his support for a four-member film crew that they wanted to send into the country to document the condition of the black rhino population. They were seeking his support so that the team would be able to safely travel around the various parks to photograph the rhinos in their natural habitat.

He and General Wesbow immediately set into motion a plan to kidnap the team and then demand five million dollars for the release of each film crew member.

A few months later when the film team arrived, they were met by a specially assigned army squad that was assigned to take them to a holding location until the ransom was paid. The kidnapping was a nonevent. A black van met the team as they exited the airport with all their equipment.

The driver and his companion helped load all the equipment and suitcases into the van and then drove to a destination outside of Nairobi where the team was to be held.

Soon after, General Mumbada learned that there was a nasty interaction with the female team leader when she insisted, they be taken to their hotel. He was told that she had a bruise that covered her right cheek where she had been backhanded. He asked for the soldiers name who had hit the leader and he also sent word that the film crew was to be treated well. He had them separated and locked in two separate rooms of the barracks where they were being held.

He and Lionel discussed how they would handle the four when the ransom was paid.

He publicly announced the film crew's abduction and said that the army was in pursuit of the kidnappers who were demanding a ransom of five million dollars per person for their safe release. He assured the news channels that the team would be found and rescued by his men.

General Ingraditi learned of the kidnapping as he listened to a news report. He was shocked by the amount of ransom that was being demanded. He was also sure that his two nemesis and strong competitors for control of the army were the ones behind the kidnapping.

He sent them a cryptic message stating, "it is not me so it must be something the two of you have cooked up. I am staying clear of it."

He was not staying clear. He set forth a plan that brought his army units closer to Nairobi in preparation of arresting both General Mumbada and General Wesbow. It seemed that the two were getting greedy and that they would no doubt think about gaining more power as well as more money.

General Mumbada and Wesbow were glad to get the message and figured that they had clear sailing and would soon be able to send a significant amount of money to their Swiss bank accounts.

They were disappointed when they news from The Society of Geographic Exploration saying that the US would not allow the organization to meet the ransom demands. This worried them but they figured it was just the first step in the ransom demand dance. They agreed that they should reiterate the ransom demand that threatened harm to the film crew if the demand was not met.

A few days later they received a reply to the ransom demand that asked how the payment should be delivered. The message was signed, Matthew Parker ransom settlement specialist.

They figured that the company had hired an outsider to deliver the ransom money.

They had never heard of a "ransom settlement specialist" but they were pleased that the ransom was to be paid. They hoped that this specialist would arrive at the airport with the ransom money where their men would quickly put this would be specialist out of business when they took control of the ransom money.

They organized a team to seize the ransom money. They had come to the conclusion that eliminating the film crew would make it easier for them to close out the kidnapping situation.

It was clear to them that their kidnapping case had grown roots and would yield the millions that they had hoped. They congratulated each other on having come up with such a lucrative idea.

They decided that a celebration outing was appropriate and visited the most expensive restaurant in Nairobi and celebrated their success.

The two would not have been celebrating if they had known who Mathew Parker was and how he solved the problems that he was assigned and the many years that he had successfully done so.

While they celebrated Mathew Parker was on his way to solve the problem they had created.

<u>3 Old Friends in Trouble</u>

What began as a trip to another great photo journalism trip to get out into the wilderness and capture the plight of the black rhino on film turned into a nightmare as soon as the team arrived in Nairobi. They had been assured they would be met with help and assistance and instead they were met by group of men they took as soldiers who loaded their things into the back of a black van and whisked them away.

Andria had her hand over the bruise on the side of her face where she had been back handed when she had demanded to be taken to the hotel where the team had reservations. It became clear to her that they had been kidnaped but she felt that a forceful approach was how to handle the situation. That aggressive approach proved to be very wrong.

She and Mary now sat in one room guarded by one of the members of the abductors. Her head ached but what she was now more worried about was Mike and Iri the two male members on her crew. She hoped that Mike would not lose his temper. He was prone to letting his anger get the best of him.

As she thought about who had lost their anger she laughed.

Her laugh seemed to bring the guard to action, and he wanted to know why she was laughing.

She answered him saying that she was just thinking about what would happen to all of the people who were involved in doing the kidnapping.

Mary sat silently across from her and with her head cupped in her hands. Mary commented that so far there was not much to laugh about. She asked how the face felt.

Andria wondered how, while coming out of the airport, they could be so easily get abducted. She figured that it was the work of whoever was in charge of the area. Clearly the abductors were in some sort of military uniform. The public aspect of where the kidnapping took place seemed to support her supposition.

She thought back to how the trip had started out. The team had been enthused when they had received their assignment to go to Kenya to the Lewa Wild Life Conservancy to film the black Rhino in its natural state. They were to produce an article about the good work being done there to repopulate the rhino population. The team had discussed the great time they all had when they filmed the documentary on elephants and then produced the story, "Of Elephants and Ivory." They figured that this story would be, "Of Rhinos and Horns."

They had gone out and celebrated their good fortune.

Andria thought about the irony that she had to hire a camera man to fill a vacancy on the team. That had been how she had first met Mathew Parker. She had hired a young camera man named Iri that Mike had taken under his tutelage to bring him up to speed.

Being kidnapped and told that they would be released when the ransom that was being asked was paid was of great concern to her. She wondered whether the company would pay the five million dollars per person that was being demanded. She hoped so. She and the team had generated one hundred times that amount with the documentary films they had produced.

That thought brought Matt back into her thinking. Matt, the person who had surprised her and the team with his escapades when they were filming, "Of Elephants and Ivory." He had demonstrated an uncanny skill at moving around within reach of the elephants that in turn seemed to accept him.

A few years later she had received some amazing film footage that she was very sure he had taken. They were amazing pictures of a myriad of fish, whales, killer whales, turtles, and manta rays. She and the team view all of it multiple times and were blown away when they watched him ride the mother whale. The were overjoyed at the close up that he got of the baby whale. Then they were more amazed when he caught a ride on the back of a killer whale and was able to get a upshot of each of the other members of that pod as each individual came up to check him out.

His shots of the gaping mouth of a shark and then a similar one of a giant Manta Ray coming straight at him had caused everyone to let out loud exclamations of surprise. She figured only Matt would have that kind of gumption and courage, but his face never made it on film.

The collection of fish and underwater scenes were beyond what the team had ever imagined could be captured on camera.

They had made that gift into a documentary that earned all of them a raise and she had received a promotion.

She wondered where Matt was and wished he were here because she was sure that he would figure out how to get all of them out of the mess they found themselves in.

Andria was soon to be surprised at the role that her "Old" friend, Mathew Parker was to play in getting her out of the mess she was in. Not only would she be surprised but she would once again be blown away with the actions he would take in accomplishing getting the team to safety.

Ian, alias Mathew Parker, had been writing one of his many fiction stories when on the news he heard the announcer discussing the kidnapping of a Geographical film crew. He immediately focused in on the report. The pictures of the film crew were that of his old friends when he had played the part of Mathew Parker and had become a camera man on the crew. He had ended up taking very close up pictures of the elephants. His problem-solving actions had temporarily ended the extensive poaching and harvesting of elephant tusks.

At that time, he was sure that his "solutions" were only temporary and that by now the poor elephants were probably in the same jam they had been in at that time.

This time his old team mates had gone to Kenya to make a similar documentary on the Black Rhinoceros. He figured this time the bad guys were more than just poachers and wheeled more power. He looked to the army to be involved.

The abduction had been on the curb of the airport when they had exited with all their equipment. Those in charge of the area must have at least looked the other way for that to happen.

He knew he would soon get his activation call. He began to think through what action he was going to take.

He was in the middle of his thought process when he got a rare call. It was a surprise in that it was his long-time handler that was on the other end of the secure line where usually it was some unknown voice that gave him the briefest and usually cryptic message possible.

His handler informed him that he was indeed being activated to solve the problem that his old friends faced.

His handler added that he had some sad news about Maurice and Ted Daimler, the two people he had saved from the Pirates off the coast of Africa. They had recently passed away within a month of each other. Their sons had inherited their furniture business, but they had left their sailing yacht, "The Lazy Lady," to him. He added that they had the boat sailed to South Africa and it was now docked at the last place where the three of them had been together.

His handler said that he was being given that information in case it would be of help in handling his new assignment.

Ian thanked him for the information and said that an idea had just popped into his mind.

There was a chuckle on the other end and his handler added "just don't kill too many of the perps," and then the line went dead.

The idea that had popped into his mind caused Ian to make a call to another old friend that he hoped would be available to help him.

Ted was sitting at home in Tampa wishing that his slow boat captaining business would come back to life. He was now known for his capabilities and was often asked to handle some of the best sailing yachts that were anchored in the Tampa Bay area but recently things had been quieter than usual. Even the occasional call to captain some of the very large power yachts had dried out.

His musings made him wonder what had happened to the person that had launched his career as the captain of the "Whistling Nanny". His career had soared after that job and a very prosperous life had followed.

When a few days later after having wondered about his long-ago acquaintance, he answered his phone and almost fell out of his chair when he heard the voice of Mathew Bitterly. It was hard for him to pay attention to what was being said because he had figured he would never hear from him again. Over the years he had come to realize that Mathew was most likely an alias for a much more clandestine profession. A profession that he still wondered about.

Once he gathered himself, he finally realized that he was being asked to Captain a yacht named the "Lazy Lady" that was currently located in South Africa. He was ecstatic.

It took him a minute to respond that it would be great to do so. He then asked what type of yacht the "Lazy Lady" happened to be. He laughed when he learned that it was a duplicate of the Whistling Nanny and replied he would love to sail her.

He took down all the information and the flight information that Matt provided. It took him several days to travel to South Africa to where the sailing yacht was moored. He decided to handle the yacht single handedly. He was impressed how the Lazy Lady looked and smelled new. It was clear that she had been refurbished. He took her out and as he put her through her paces the years melted away and it seemed like only yesterday when he and Matt had sailed the Whistling Nanny.

Once he had the yacht underway to Mombasa, he let Matt know.

Ian, now Matt, was figuring out how he could get out to the field and make contact as soon as possible. He had been given the phone connection with the kidnappers, so he decided to become the person who was to finalize the ransom negotiations with them.

He placed the call and conveyed the fact that the company was sending him out with the ransom money in cash and that he would deliver it and would hand it over when the four abductees were released to him.

The ease with which the kidnappers agreed and gave him the location where the exchange was to take place let him know that it was a set up and that he and the four would be killed when they tried to leave that location. He also figured he might be stopped at the airport just as Andrea had been.

He of course did not have any connection with the company that Andria and her team worked for and the money to be used for the ransom was coming out of his bottomless offshore account that he had used for more than thirty years. It was an account that always had a minimum of one million dollars in it but had access to whatever amount he needed. The amount of money that he had withdrawn for this problem-solving session was not the highest, but it was close. He wondered what the person managing the bank account thought when he withdrew these large sums of money.

He decided to get into the Kenya surreptitiously. He flew into Dar es Salaam in Tanzania. From there he flew on a private charter into Nairobi where it landed on a private airfield.

He arrived several days earlier than he had shared with the abductors. He wanted time to walk through the situation he would face.

He scouted out the exchange location so he could figure out how to counter act what he knew would be a trap.

He went to the specified location and decided to take the position nearest to the statue in the park where the exchange was to take place. It had a wide area to the front of a statue of Absko Njeri, who had saved the country and had guided it throughout his life time. Ian noted that the life time was very short since Absko died at the age of forty-one. He took the location as a signal that he needed to be able to control the situation so that he would not follow Absko.

There was a large flat brick covered area out in front of the statue, and it had a long set of stairs behind the statue that went down about a football field in length to a lower parking area.

He called his support team and requested the delivery of sixty bars of radio controlled fused C4 with a remote-control App for his phone that could be used to trigger the C4. He said he needed the order in the next twelve-four hours and that the order was to be placed in the bushes behind the statue.

The next night, he placed C4 in a semi-circle under the bricks out about fifty feet, and another semi-circle closer in at thirty feet. He then went out in the cobble stone street and placed C4 where the trucks or vehicles would park. He then placed the C4 down the sides of the steps coming up from the lower parking lot. He set up a trip wire near the top of the steps but counted on the ability to set off the C4 via his phone.

He made sure that the statue base would provide the cover that would be needed when he set the C4 off.

He hid the money that he was to exchange in bushes just behind the statue.

It was near morning when he finished setting everything up.

He then went to the airport so he could make it appear that he had come in as per his instructions.

At the airport he found his way in through a service area and went to a set of lockers where four empty suitcases were located and strapped the four together. The four cases were the same as the ones with the money in them that were back at the statue. Each case had its own set of wheels which would carry them toward the kidnappers as the exchange happened. His empty ones were already carrying C4 in them that were timer controlled.

He went to the curb and got into a cab that was at the back of the long cab que line.

The driver was about to refuse him, but the hundred-dollar bill Ian held out to him caused him to smile and ask where he wanted to go.

Ian gave him the location and the driver pulled away from the curb.

Ian looked back to see if they were being followed and was relieved that they were not. He was sure that by jumping the line he had gotten away from whomever had been sent to meet him and most likely take the money they thought he would be carrying.

He paid the driver during the transit and asked him to drive up to the statue and then leave immediately.

He had just gotten the money cases, the empty cases arranged, and his phone app activated when a large black SUV followed by two armed trucks came roaring into the area in front of the statue.

Ian watched as they parked exactly where he had hoped they would. Once they parked at least thirty soldiers lined up in front of the lead SUV.

Ian thought about his handlers comment about how many people he shouldn't kill and now wondered how many he would.

Two men dress impeccably in black suites sporting white boutonnières addressed him with a bull horn.

Ian replied with a much smaller voice amplifier and warned them not to send the troops up the back way and to keep the troops out front at least twenty meters away from the statue.

He then pointed to the four cases that he had brought out and said that each had five million dollars in them. He then rolled three of the cases back behind the statue.

He suggested they get the exchange under way.

He watched as one of the two men in black communicated with someone that was remotely located.

Ian hoped it was to keep the men in the lower parking lot from coming up the stairs. He backed up to the point where he could take a quick look down and was pleased to see the steps were empty.

He watched the other leader call back to a person standing by the side back door to the SUV.

The door was opened, and Mike stepped out and reached in to help Mary exit. Then a young man that Ian would later learn was Iri stepped out and reached and helped Andria out.

Ian could see the bruise that colored one side of her face and knew that she had angered someone.

He asked that she be the first to be sent across to him.

One of the men in black as Ian now thought of the two, said they would determine the order of the exchange. He pushed Mary to the front and asked for the first five million dollars.

Ian replied that when she made it to the statue, he would push the first case with the money across. He was pleased to see that Mary was given a push and began walking across.

When she was at the statue, Ian simultaneously pushed her behind the statue and pushed the first suitcase toward the two men in charge.

He then pulled a second suitcase to the side of the statue.

He asked Mary to keep her eyes on the stairs and let him know if anybody was coming up.

The first suitcase was opened to make sure that the money was inside.

Ian made the point that he was keeping his end of the bargain and that they should continue the exchange.

Mike was the next to be sent across.

When he reached the statue, Ian again pushed a suitcase with the money across.

It was again checked.

Ian told Mike to get the weapons out of the bushes and get ready to fight for his life. He was glad to hear Mike say he was ready to take down as many as he could.

Ian was surprised when the two in charge said they would send both the remaining persons across together and that he should push the last two cases to them.

He figured that immediately after this exchange the action would start.

Ian went behind the statue and selected two empty cases that were loaded with the C4 versus.

He waited until Andria and Iri were near him and then reached down and activated the C4 timers in the empty suit cases and pushed them towards the kidnapers and at the same time shoved the two behind the statue as the anticipated gun fire from the group of soldiers began.

He was hit but his body armor saved him.

He lay down and took out both of the men in black and watched as the two suitcases exploded and leveled the first line of soldiers.

The next line of soldiers ran forward firing their weapons.

When they reached the most distant ring of C4 he set that ring off and eliminated the second wave. The third wave was getting ready to follow one of the trucks that had a fifty-caliber machine gun mounted on it when Ian set the C4 under it off and lifted the truck several feet into the air before it blew up from whatever ammunition it was carrying.

The carnage was not complete. The remaining soldiers ran toward the statue. They all reached the thirty-foot ring of explosives and were totally annihilated when Ian set that group of C4 explosives off.

Mike was shouting that the troops from below were running up the stairs.

Ian went to where Mike was shooting downward taking out the lead soldiers. He told him to let them come up.

Mike looked at him and asked if, he was sure.

Ian smiled and said that he wanted all the soldiers from the parking lot to make it onto the stairs.

He asked Mike to guard his back and make sure there were no survivors in front of the statue.

He waited until the stairs were full and then he set off the line of explosive charges he had put on each side of the stairs.

Andria shook her head and thanked him for coming to save their bacon. She commented that he was delivering the carnage that in her anger she had dreamt of.

Ian smiled and replied that he would love to catch up on old times, but they needed to make their escape.

He went out to where the suit cases with the five million dollars were sitting and pulled them to the back of the statue.

He pulled the other two with money in them and place all four together.

He asked each of the team to carry their own five million dollars and to follow him to the van in front of the statue.

Andria laughed when she realized she had been traded for with an empty case loaded not with money but with C4. She commented that Matt was a true gambler.

Ian said that he had the cases with the actual money ready to go if each case continued to be examined. He had made the switch at the last moment when the kidnap leaders had suggested sending over two cases at once.

He chuckled and ask if she had a problem with how he gambled since it had worked out so well.

<u>*4 Race through the City*</u>

*I*an asked if they should take the black SUV.

Andria immediately said they should because it had all the camera equipment in it.

Mary spoke up and commented that it had comfortable seats.

Mike added that he thought it was bullet proofed.

Ian looked across the area at all the bodies and cringed at the carnage he had caused. He remembered his handler's comment about not killing too many of the abductors. So far, he had started out with a huge body count, and he was not yet out of Kenya. He was sure that none of the soldiers had expected to be mowed down by the brick and stone shrapnel caused by the explosions.

He asked everyone to select a weapon and pick up as much ammunition as possible as they made their way across to the SUV.

He went to where the two men in black suits were laying and picked up one of the phones. He hoped to be able to listen to the field communications of those that would come to the scene.

He picked up several of the rifles and was very pleased that one was a sniper's rifle. He stopped and checked it out and as he was picking up the bag of ammunition for it that the soldier had carried, he realized that the soldier had a case on his shoulder that held the scope for the rifle.

Ian figured that the find of a sniper's rifle might well be worth more than the money that he had brought for the ransom. It might well be the weapon that would save them.

He turned the van around and headed back the way the kidnapers had driven in. At the first intersection he took a right and just as he was about to make a left at the next intersection, he saw a convoy of soldiers speeding in toward the statue area. He knew that he had been very lucky with the departure timing. He made the left and then at the next intersection he took a right. He kept up his zig-zagging route up for several miles. Then at what seemed to be a major road he headed southeast. His goal was to get out of Kenya and to do so he needed to get to Mombasa where he had sent Ted with the Lazy Lady. He knew that he had to get out as quickly as possible because of the carnage he had left behind. He was beginning to suspect that it was the army that was in charge of staging the kidnaping.

Everybody in the SUV had been quiet since they had driven out of Nairobi. Then he had to divert from going south because he saw a roadblock where the military were checking out cars. He immediately took a small east bound road and drove away from that area.

This, however, put them well away from the direction he had hoped to be going. What made it worse was that the road was taking him east by northeast which was taking him farther away from where he wanted to go.

Getting food supplies and then finding a place to get some rest was what he figured needed to happen next.

He looked on the map and decided to go to Ol Donyo Sabuk National Park where he hoped they would be able to stop for the night. He knew he had to stay out of sight for the next few days.

A large grocery store in the suburbs caught his eye and he stopped there. He asked Mary and Iri to go in and get enough food for a week. He suggested that they get a variety of food that did not need to be refrigerated or kept cold but would fit everyone's appetite. He added they should get plenty of water and a variety of soft drinks.

He set out to obtain a new license plate. He found a screw driver in a tool box in the back of the SUV.

He had asked Andria and Mike to stay in the van but keep a look out in case they were being followed.

He removed the license plate on the SUV and went out hunting for a new one. He found a van parked by a dumpster that provided him the opportunity to switch plates.

Mary and Iri where just coming out of the grocery store pushing two fully loaded grocery carts when he returned. Iri was wearing a large brimmed, grass woven hat.

Ian knew that such a hat would be great if he were out in the hot Kenyon sun. He asked Iri to go back in and buy one for him.

Once Iri was back and they were all in, he asked Mike to drive so he could think through how they were going to get out of the country.

Andria shook her head and commented that she wondered who he really was, but she was so happy to see him that it really didn't matter who he was.

Ian, i.e. Matt, smiled and said that he was the problem-solver that had come to the aid of his old friends to solve their problem.

Iri commented that he was glad to have him as a friend.

Mike drove down a long dirt road into the middle of the park.

Every few miles Ian had Mike pull under the cover of a large oak or maple-like tree to put the van out of sight. On one such occurrence a helicopter flew by overhead confirming that there was an all-out search for them.

Deep into the park Ian directed Mike to a stand of trees that overlooked a small lake and had him pull well under the trees so that the van was not visible from the sky. He did not want it spotted from the air.

He opened one of the empty money cases to see if there was anything in the case that might be of use. He first defused the C4 and then examined the case. He found that the case was lined with a wire mesh. He figured that it was meant to keep the money from being detected.

The wire gauge was heavy enough that by folding it and doubling the wire, it was strong enough to serve as a fishhook. He then unwove part of the mesh to form a long continuous wire that was more than twenty feet long.

He decided that he was going to go fishing.

He looked down to the lake and was pleased to see weeping willow trees lining the lake bank. He saw several that were just right to become a fishing pole.

He found a box knife in the toolbox and walked with his line and his hook and led the way to where he saw a young slender willow that he felt was long enough to serve as a pole. He cut the small tree down and trimmed off the small limbs and leaves and created a clean ten-foot pole. He then looked around for something to serve as a bobber and for some sort of bait.

Mike walked over to a large flat stone and lifted it to expose a large number of very large ants tending to large plump larvae. He carefully picked up about a dozen and gently put the rock back in place.

Andria found a dry round seed pot and tested it out in the water. It floated, so she brought it over to Matt.

Ian took the seed pod and with a short piece of wire attached it to his line.

He accepted two ant larvae and put them on the hook.

He walked to the edge of the lake and threw his line out. He was surprised when almost immediately the bobber went under, and his pole bent.

He played the fish slowly in toward the shore and then walked backward uphill and dragged the fish up on the shore where both Andria and Mike worked together to capture it. It was a beauty that was about as long as Andrea's combined forearm and hand.

The sun reflecting off the scales made the top fins glisten a purple and black color and the scales formed a mesh of white and black that looked much like the mesh that had lined the money suitcase.

It would make a fine meal.

Mike commented that it was large enough that once grilled they would all be able to have a nice piece.

Ian suggested they try for another so that everyone could get a larger portion of fish.

Fishing seemed to release the tension that had embraced the group. Everyone tried their hand and without exception they all caught one.

It was clear that it had been a long time since anyone had fished on the lake.

Iri caught the biggest fish which turned out to be a huge catfish that had been sucking on his hook but had not given any hint of being on the line until Iri tried to pull his pole out of the water. He thought he had hooked a stump or had snagged his line on rocks on the bottom of the lake. He walked backward up the slope away from the lake and was surprised when the catfish started to fight to keep from getting pulled out.

It took him, Mike, and Andrea to get the fish up the slope.

Ian liked how the team had come back to life. They sat around and grilled fish on a variety of sticks that they had retrieved and made into skewers.

He listened as each of them shared a fishing story or gave advice on the best seasoning to bring out the flavor of a fish. He preferred his simple routine of salting the fish after each bite and putting it back out over the fire while he was chewing on the bite he had taken.

He had already decided where he was going to sleep. He pointed to a limb of a giant native silky oak that was about one hundred feet away from where the van was located. He suggest that Andrea and Mary fold the two back seats as flat as possible and that Iri was most likely short enough to be comfortable in the very back of the SUV.

He pointed Mike to another limb in the silky oak, but Mike said he preferred to incline the passenger's seat as far back as possible and sleep there.

Ian stripped the seat cover from the SUV's back seat and climbed into the tree and lay with his feet against the trunk and relaxed along the slight incline of the limb.

The night temperature dropped down to a cool fifty degrees. The temperature in the van dropped down to a comfortable level. Ian was glad to have the hat to cover his head to keep the dew off his face.

He woke up early and decided to see what he could find around the camp.

About halfway around the lake, he came across a black rhino family.

The bull was huge.

His horn was a beautiful black two-foot curved sickle-shaped arc that looked like it came to a very sharp point.

The cow was about two thirds his size and had a short stubby horn. She was shadowed by a calf that was about the size of a yearling cow.

He knew immediately what he was going to do.

He returned to camp and woke up the team and said they should grab the camera equipment and follow him because he had a surprise.

He took out his personal hand held, reflex lens digital camera and led the way to where the rhino family was located.

He spotted some droppings and decided to use the trick that had worked so well when he had put elephant manure on his clothing to get in close with the elephants. Once he had rubbed the harder rhino dropping on his clothes, he slowly walked out away from the tree that he had been hiding behind.

He wanted to get close enough to get some really close up shots that he knew Mary would like. As she referred to them as, "shots that made it easy to edit."

The cow must have seen his movement and walked slowly toward him. He was ready to bolt for the tree, if necessary, but he stood still. After a moment she snorted and turned away to take a bite of some green grass. The baby rhino came much closer but when it sniffed Ian it too turned away and went to its mother. It had come right up to him, and he knew that he had some great shots of the little one.

He followed the three as the bull led the way to a shady spot under a huge oak tree and lay down. The cow did the same and the little one pushed his nose between her legs to get his morning meal. The cow obligingly raised one leg so that her two tits were available to her calf.

Ian made his way slowly around the three and got close ups from his three hundred sixty excruciatingly slow walk.

When he got back to the tree trunk, he stepped behind it and took a deep breath. He made a production of lifting his camera lens cover in the air and displayed it to Andrea and then put it on. This was an old joke that went back to the time when they filmed the elephants.

He walked away from the scene keeping the large tree trunk between he and the three rhinos. Once he felt he was far enough away he turned and walked back to where the rest of the team was situated.

He handed Mary his camera and said that the pictures were hers, but he wanted his camera back.

Mary commented that with his and Mike's pictures she would be able to produce an entire set of pictures and that once she mixed in some shots that she had from other excursions she would be able to put together an entire story.

Andria commented on how crazy he still was but that she was sure his close ups would save the trip from being a total loss. She then held her nose and commented that he really needed to take a bath.

Back on the army airfield two side gunners, the pilot and co-pilot were just lifting off as the film team was out filming the rhinos. They had been given the coordinates where they would find the van with the group fleeing the army.

The pilot commented that it was going to be like shooting sitting ducks. He was homing in on the beacon that was sending out a strong signal.

He was flying in low and fast.

The two gunners were arguing with which one of them should get to have their side facing the van and be first to take out the people on the ground.

The pilot laughed and said he would give each of them equal time shooting the sitting ducks.

He was coming in low and at his top speed.

He began his first pass and as he took a long slow turn to the left to give his favorite gunner the first pass.

Suddenly his oil level gauge alarmed, and he saw dark grey smoke bellowing from the engine compartment.

He realized the chopper had been hit. He hoped desperately that he would be able to make it back to the airfield.

Little did he realize that he would make it less than halfway back when the engine would freeze, and the rotors would stop. His expertise saved the crew but all of them were injured when he brought it down for a hard landing.

When Ian got back to the van, he took out a light jogging outfit and walked down to the lake where he stripped down and carried all of clothes into the lake with him. After getting out and putting on his jogging outfit he spread his clothes out on some bushes to dry.

He returned to the van and was getting his suitcase organized when he heard the sound of a helicopter.

He looked up and barely visible on the horizon he could see the dark green of what he figured was a military helicopter coming directly toward them.

He assembled his sniper's rifle and took a position under the oak tree and looked through his scope. It was clear to him that it was indeed coming straight at them.

He waited until the chopper was just within the range of his sniper's rifle and to the point that he felt comfortable to shoot. He was trying to incapacitate the copter in such a fashion that it would need to return to some place where it could safely land.

His first shot hit but it did not do what Ian wanted it to do.

The second shot hit the engine compartment and must have hit the oil pan or done some other damage because smoke started coming out of the compartment.

The helicopter turned and went back along the route that it had come.

Ian shouted that it was time for them to leave. He ran down and rescued his clothes and returned to the van.

He asked that they all check the van to see if they could find a tracking device. Mike was the one that found it attached to the top of the back wheel well on the driver's side. He was able to pull it off.

He asked how Ian had known that there would be one.

Ian responded that the helicopter was coming straight at them and must have been following a signal.

Ian trimmed the two-sided tape on the tracking device and said he would be back shortly. He instructed the team to get ready to leave.

He jogged back to where the rhinos were still napping. He boldly walk to the back of the bull and clued the tracking device to his back haunch. He figured it would stay in place for a couple of days and then would drop off.

He jogged back to the van and had Mike take a small road that went directly east.

The small road seemed to go on forever.

During the transit Ian put in a call to his support team and requested a new transport.

He specified that it be white, bullet proof, have tinted windows all around and have comfortable seating for five.

Andrea laughed and asked what kind of rental company offered delivery services in the Keyan outback.

After several hours Ian was beginning to worry when the small road ended in a large parking lot where there were several vans and other cars that were mostly parked under the trees around the lot and not in the parking spaces so they could be in the shade. Ian pointed to a white SUV on the other side of the lot parked in a spot that was on the lot but in the shade of a huge tree.

Andrea commented that she could not believe that he had ordered a specific vehicle in the middle of an isolated park and a few hours later had it waiting for him and conveniently parked in the shade.

He had Mike pull up parallel to it and they transferred all their belongings into their new transport.

He then put the black SUV farther under the large tree so that it would be hard to spot from the air.

Mike commented on how much better their new SUV drove.

Everyone else made some sort of comment about its comfort and the great view they now enjoyed.

Back at the army airfield the command was shocked to get the mayday call from the helicopter that had been sent out to eliminate the escaping film crew.

The command group had been expecting a successful kill report and had a site cleanup crew standing by to be sent to the location to clean up the carnage. Instead, they sent out an ambulance to the coordinates sent in by the copter pilot.

They decided to send out the new gunship helicopter that sported a gatling gun. It had arrived at the beginning of the month and had yet to see action in the field. They assigned all three pilots trained to fly it to take it out and find the van by homing in on the tracking signal.

Shortly after the chopper left the field, they called back to say that the signal had led them to a rhinoceros that was standing in the middle of the forest.

A variety of theories of how the tracking device could possibly end up on a rhino ensued.

Everyone knew that some brave or very stupid person had to be responsible.

When the airfield commander called General Mumbada he was told to have the helicopter search the highway for an SUV or large vehicle going south to Mombasa and take out any vehicle capable of carrying five people and a be able to carry a significant amount of luggage.

The order was sent out and the gunship went towards the highway.

The pilots was enjoying taking the new gunship into action. The three carried on a continuous chatter about how great it felt.

They had all qualified on the gunship and were eager to see how it performed in actual combat. They viewed their current assignment well short of combat but figured it would give them the feel of how it could take out their chosen target.

The pilot pointed to white SUV driving south toward Mombasa. It was the only vehicle for as far as any of them could see so they agreed that they should take it out. They swooped in and the gatling gun put out a stream of bullets that hit the passenger side but amazingly did not stop the vehicle.

The pilot radioed in that they had found their target, and he was going in for the kill.

He took a long sweep around and lined up for the kill shot. He was surprised when he tried to fire, and the gatling gun seemed to disintegrate and send shrapnel back at the window. He was just about to swing away when he saw a star-shaped hole appeared in the window in front of him, and the pain in his chest caused him to lean forward. He watched in amazement as the highway seemed to be coming toward him as his vision slowly ceased.

Periodically Ian would stand up through the sunroof and scan the horizon. He did this every fifteen or twenty minutes and thought that perhaps they would not be found but about three quarters of the way towards Mombasa he spotted a helicopter making its approach. Looking through his sniper scope, he realized that it was one of the newer gunships that sported a fifty-caliber gatling gun that fired six thousand rounds per minute.

The sight of such a formidable craft cause his veins to run cold. He knew they were in deep trouble.

He let everyone know that they were about to be attacked.

He asked Iri to hand him a bullet every time he put his hand back for one. He then stood up and positioned himself.

He told Mike to zig zag down the road and to constantly change speed.

The Helio got one round off and hit the SUV on the passenger door and cracked the bullet proof window next to where Andrea was sitting.

Ian fired three shots at the barrel section of the gatling gun as it came in for a second round. He then put three shots through the window and took out the pilot. It appeared that the Helio was going to crash directly into them.

He shouted to Mike to gun it and go straight down the highway.

He watched as the Helio hit the edge of the highway directly behind them, slid across and then blew up when it went into the ditch.

Andria sat back up straight and then touched the cracked bullet proof window and commented that if she lived to tell the story of the filming of the Black Rhino, she would add the adventure that she and her team had so far lived through.

Ian smiled and asked if it would be as good as her last two documentaries.

Andria smiled and said that the last footage of whales, dolphins and Orcas that he had sent her had gotten the team raises and she had been promoted.

This time she was only hoping to make it out alive.

Ian nodded and said that alive would be good.

He then said they would need to change their mode of transportation but this time they would need to do it the old-fashioned way and stop at some car lot and buy whatever they could so they could continue to the coast.

He had Mike stop at the first lot that they found where there were several cars on the lot.

There was one newer pickup that had an extended cab that fit the bill. The camera equipment and luggage was put in the back and a tarp was put over all of it. The cab was roomy enough that everyone was comfortable.

The lot owner asked about the SUV and Ian said that it was his to keep but that he should take it to the repair shop to have the passenger door repaired and suggested that he change the color of the SUV as well.

The owner smiled, nodded and seemed to understand that the van was hot.

They arrived to Mumbada and drove to where the Lazy Lady was anchored just off the beach.

After all the luggage and equipment was off loaded, Ian said that he had business that needed finishing in Nairobi, and he was driving there and would return when that was over.

It was about a five-hour drive, and he arrived there early in the morning.

5 General's Greed

General Mumbada was furious that he had lost more than forty men and two helicopters to whomever had come to the rescue of the kidnapped film crew. He had just purchased the helicopter gunship that had been shot down at a cost of fifty million dollars. He had been planning to use it if and when he decided to take over the country. He pounded his desk and shout out, "fifty million dollars. I want the head of the person who shot it down." He now faced not only the loss of many men and two invaluable helicopters, but he was also out of the twenty million dollars ransom.

How the exchange of the prisoners for the twenty million dollars could have gone so wrong was beyond comprehension. The carnage out in front of the statue and on the steps down to the lower parking lot had shocked and astounded him. He had been in some battles, but he had never seen so many bodies in such a small space.

He had been told a moment prior to the carnage that there was only one person present with the ransom money.

He thought that if he had a few people like him in his army he could take over Kenya and the rest of Africa. He wondered how one person could possibly have done so much damaged but worse he had gotten away with both the kidnapped people and the money. He had left a trail of death and destruction that shocked both he and Lionel, his second in command.

His men had found the tracking device that he had planted on the black SUV out in the middle of the Ol Donyo Sabuk National Park reserve. Later they found the black van abandoned miles away parked under a tree just off the normal parking lot used by hikers.

He had sent out his prized new gunship to look for any cars that were heading south on B8. It had found one and had gone in for the kill. But later he learned that it had somehow been shot out of the sky.

A gunship that he knew was one of the most formidable weapons in the sky had been brought down by someone in the SUV!

He could only believe it was the same person who had caused the carnage at the ransom exchange.

It all seemed impossible.

He slammed his hand down on his desk and shouted out in anger.

He and Lional discussed how they might still capture this mysterious, deadly person and decided to monitor the coast for any major navy vessel that might be waiting for this person.

They set up a meeting with the General of the Airforce to get him to cruise the coast to check for any foreign naval vessels or any smaller boats making their way away from the port of Mombasa.

Some how they needed to eliminate this destroyer of their well laid plans.

He was also worried about what General Ingraditi might do to take advantage of the situation.

As it turned out General Mumbada had a right to be worried.

General Ingraditi was indeed monitoring the situation. He had gone to the square where all the bodies of the dead soldiers were still being removed. He walked the area and realized that whoever had orchestrated the events that took place was a formidable adversary that if left alone might solve his problem with his two adversary generals who had gone well beyond what was acceptable for anyone in the army.

They would need to be dealt with, but he figured it was worth waiting to see how much more they would lose trying to carry out their current kidnapping scheme.

A short time later, his informant reported that two helicopters had been lost in pursuit of the escaped camera crew. He knew that one was the newest gunships that the army had acquired at an exceedingly high cost that he had objected to.

This cemented his decision to standby and monitor what took place.

Ian arrived in Nairobi in the wee hours of the morning. On the way he had called his support group and asked for the name of the person who was in charge of the army that controlled Nairobi and what his normal daily schedule was. He also asked for information about the person second in command, and he wanted pictures of both.

The information came back to him as he drove into Nairobi. He drove to the work address he had been given. It was an old colonial structure that looked like a library with four columns out front. It had a large loop in front that came in directly from a main thoroughfare. A block away to one side there were tall glass front, glimmering business office buildings.

As he looked around, he realized that there was only one two story building on the other side that might provide him a place to shoot from.

The taller buildings on the other side of the circle were all better sniper locations, but he figured they would be traps for him because he would have to come down several stories and then exit into very busy streets. The much smaller building would make the shot extremely difficult, but he would be able to depart in seconds and drive away in a direction that would not expose him.

He drove to the smaller three-story building and entered the parking lot in back and then he drove his escape route. He found a large bus station where he could abandon his pickup in a multilevel parking lot that was down the street from the station.

He went into the bus station and bought two tickets. One to Kampala to the west and another to Mombasa in the south. He wanted to be able to openly get on the bus to Kampala, get off of it once it had gone a few blocks and then come back and get on the bus going to Mombasa. He hoped that action would for a short time misdirect anyone that might be trying to track him.

He then returned to the two-story building and sighted in his rifle for the range that he would be shooting across.

The rifle had a silencer, so he took a practice shop at a red soft drink can that was illuminated by the street light. The can flew up into the air and let him know that his shot came in a little low.

He figured he had just enough height to shoot over the heads of the guards that he was sure would surround the general. His target was the general and he didn't want to hit one of the soldiers.

It would need to be one of his better shots.

He then napped through most of the early morning but was up early to monitor the situation in front of the general's office building. It remained quiet throughout the early morning until people began arriving for work.

He arranged his bullets so he could take several shots if necessary.

He had concluded that it would be too dangerous for him to take the rifle with him, so he planned to abandon everything on the roof when he left.

He was not worried about leaving the evidence behind. In fact, he figured it would create work that would cause any decision makers to wait to get what they believed to be critical information and then they would be confused when they found no fingerprints on the weapon and learned the weapon belonged to one of the dead soldiers killed in front of the statue during the ransom exchange.

He watched as a black limo, followed by a military truck with a mounted fifty-caliber machine gun, entered the square.

He loaded his rifle and got ready.

He watched as six soldiers stood three on each side of the limo's back door as it was opened.

His peripheral vision caught a similar limo also followed by an armored truck entering and parking behind the first two vehicles.

He kept his eyes on the first limo and the person stepping out from it. When that person was totally out, and he verified their identity, he slowly squeezed the trigger.

He did not wait to see what had happened but automatically reloaded.

He raised his scope to catch the second person getting out of the second limo. He verified that it was the second person he had on his short list of two. He followed the same procedure and watched as a second shot successfully found the target.

His shots had been silent, his location at the top of the less-than-ideal building had proved to be the best one for him. There was no return gunfire.

He made his move to escape.
One thousand and one.

He put everything down and crawled across the roof.

One thousand and two.

One thousand and three.

One thousand and four

He was to the back to the fire escape.

One thousand five.

He slid down the fire escape

One thousand six.

He got into the pickup, started it.

One thousand seven.

One thousand eight.

One thousand nine.

He drove away.

One thousand ten.

He took a deep breath and thought, "get away time ten seconds."

He drove to the bus station, went past it and turned into the public parking garage across the street and parked his pickup in a back far corner, got out and walked back to the bus station where the bus to Kampala was just loading.

He handed the bus driver his ticket and took the first seat behind him and put his overnight bag on his lap.

He chatted with the bus driver letting him know that he was going to his brother's wedding.

The bus left the station and two blocks later, he let out a loud groan and explained that he needed to get off because he had left his wallet in his car.

The bus driver stopped to let him off but said that he could not refund the ticket and that would need to be done at the station.

Ian thanked him for stopping and giving him the information and gave him a tip.

He then got out and casually walked back to the station and got on the bus that would go to Mombasa. This time he took one of the back seats near the back door.

After the bus was on the way, Ian placed a call to his support team and put in an order for the armament he wanted to take on board the Lazy Lady.

He then put his seat back and fell asleep.

The bus stopped for lunch, and he had a half of a grilled chicken with a side of French fries, took a short walk and then got back on the bus.

He had called ahead to let Ted know that he was on the way and would arrive late in the afternoon and that he would have a significant amount luggage to bring on board.

General Ingraditi learned about the assassination of Generals Mumbada and Wesbow and moved immediately to take firm command of their sections of the Army. He sent out communiques to all the military leaders announcing his consolidation of the Army under his command.

He visited the offices of both Mumbada and Wesbow and noted their proud display of their graduation degrees.

He smiled as he thought about the fact that they had gone to the next world as number one followed by number two.

It was the order that the two had gone throughout their lives. He was sure this time their greed had led them to make choices that had resulted in their one-two demise. They had underestimated a very deadly opponent.

He had no plans to pursue that person and hoped that he and the team of photographers would leave the country. He was sure that the person that had come to their rescue had also come with the means of escape, and he had no plans to get in the way.

Ted shared the news with the rest of the team that Matt was on his way back and that he had asked that he be prepared to bring a fair amount of luggage on board.

Andrea commented that the luggage that Matt was talking about would most likely be weapons.

Ted shared the fact that he had captained for Matt several years earlier and the only weapon he had ever seen him use was a camera.

Andrea laughed and said that Matt had always been the best with whatever weapon he had in his hands and that he used his camera with the same expertise that she was sure he could use whatever weapon he had in his hands.

She added that she had now witnessed what he could do under almost any situation and figured him to be one of the world's most deadly, dangerous, gentle, friendly persons she had ever met.

She asked if anyone wanted to bet on what Matt's luggage would be.

Ian arrived in Mombasa and left the bus station and got in a taxi. He got a call that his order was at the location he had specified.

He had the taxi driver drop him off in the beach side parking lot entrance and after paying him he walked toward the pile that he saw just past the far end at of the parking lot.

He took inventory and found that he was short one shoulder grenade launcher. A note on the pile explained that they had not been able to get a third one in the time frame he had specified. They had augmented the number of grenades for the grenade launchers.

He called Ted to pick him up.

Once all the boxes were brought on board he asked if supper was yet to be served because he was starving.

Mary said that they were having a pepperoni-cheese pizza with extra cheese that would be out of the oven in a few moments. She added that she had made a small side salad and a large pitcher of tea to round things out.

Andrea asked if whatever he had gone back to Nairobi to address had been resolved successfully.

Ian nodded and said that he figured their trouble with being hunted was over.

Andrea asked if that was the case why had he brought enough fire power on board to take on a fleet of ships.

Ian smiled and asked why she thought it was armament.

She laughed and said because what was in each box was boldly written on its exterior.

Ted had listened to the exchange and realized that he was seeing another side of Matt that he had not seen on their first time together.

He wondered what Matt had been up to when they had sailed the Whistling Nanny and then he remembered the gigantic explosion as they left the harbor in Ensenada. He now wondered if Matt had something to do with that explosion that had been unbelievably loud even a mile out to sea.

Ian ate his pizza and afterwards went up on the deck and proceeded to unpack the various weapons.

He put the two self-propelled grenade launchers and the extra grenades at the very back of the yacht.

He then unpacked his new sniper's rifle, assembled it and then tried several shots out at stones he saw on the beach.

Andrea and the rest of the team watched and were amazed at how good he was.

Once he was satisfied, he unpacked a series of weapons for each person on board.

He threw out several plastic bottles and asked everyone to shoot at the bottles. He took note that Mike and Ted were proficient with the rifles they had chosen. The rest were able to get a few shots close to the bottles with varied success.

He figured he had two capable marksmen, and the rest were willing shooters.

He thought about the saying, "you make tea with the leaves you have on hand."

In this case he had to make do with the army that was on board the Lazy Lady.

He asked Ted to take the packing material to the beach and to pick up the target bottles on the way.

He then explained that he was preparing to interact with the coastal pirates that would most probably try to take them as hostages for ransom and the Lazy Lady as a prize.

Andria commented that the trip to film black rhinos seemed to have a continuous set of twists and turns that tested their survival skills.

It seemed to her that they had just gotten out of the frying pan but had jumped into the fire. She added that she did not want to be hostage to any other Africans, pirates or otherwise.

Ian smiled and commented that she was the one that had signed the filming contract. He then asked if she had read the fine print to see if it had a "do not kidnap or no pirates allowed clause" that she might have missed.

She nodded and said that she had not read her contract that carefully.

6 Pirates

General Ingraditi reviewed the arial panoramic stream of images that his helicopter had captured of the short but dramatic battle between the four pirate vessels and a single sailing yacht of about the same size.

He was sure he was now seeing the actions of the same individual who had vanquished more than forty attacking soldiers, had taken down two helicopters and had so efficiently assassinated Generals Mumbada and Wesbow.

The report about the assassination had stated that it had taken almost an hour to find the location of where the shots had been taken because the assumption was that a sniper would have chosen one of the tall buildings that allowed for a clear direct shot.

The folks in the field explained that shooting from the three-story building put the two shots in the extremely lucky category.

The general figured that there was nothing about luck that was involved. It had not been luck that had so far ensured the escape of the camera crew and whoever was rescuing them.

Now as he reviewed the footage coming in from his helicopter that was flying along the coast, he was not surprised so much as he was amazed.

He marveled at the first bomb that was clearly a homemade device being hurdled at the first boat and was taken by surprise at seeing the boat seemingly stand on its nose and drive itself half way down into the water. The second and third boats each suffered a similar fate. The fourth boat stopped to pick up the few survivors that were in the water.

He knew these were not novice pirates but ones that had in the past attacked and taken over huge merchant ships and held them for ransom. It was clear they had not expected to face the type of defensive actions that devastated them. The fourth attack ship had stopped to rescue the pirates on the first three boats. The boats did not sink and would most likely be salvaged.

The unscathed yacht sailed on.

He knew that his decision to discontinue having the army pursue the film crew had been the correct one. He was sure that he would need to mend some political fences as part of resolving the whole kidnapping incident but that was a small price to pay for now having complete control of the army and subsequently the entire country.

He knew he would be able to lay the blame on two deceased generals.

He was now the top dog, or as many Kenyans would say the Pride's Male Lion. He would make sure that he would be Kenya's Lion.

He took the initiative to leak key portions of the video of the pirate attack as a means of closing the chapter of what had happened in Kenya.

On the morning after they left Mombasa Ian saw the approaching pirates. He realized that there were four large high-speed boats and that he would need more firepower than he had laid out.

He figured he would not have time to reload a rocket launcher, so he retrieved a block of C4 and carefully wrapped a nylon cord around it that extended out about three feet.

He cut a foot off a broomstick and tied the cord to it. This would allow him to swing the C4 in a loop and then release the entire contrivance as he launched it at the bow of the nearest of the oncoming boats.

He decided to use the homemade bomb first and then follow up with the self-propelled grenades.

The rate at which the boats were closing in surprised him. He asked Ted to take the Lazy Lady to its top speed and make rather wide zig zags so he could get the oncoming boats to close in close to each other as they pursued them.

He asked Mike to standby in case a pirate got on board. He suggested everyone else go below.

As the boats closed in, he watched as the boat that had been in the lead for some reason dropped back.

Ian had no way of knowing that the captain of that lead boat had seen something that brought back the memory of the horrible explosion that had wiped out most of the members of the group of pirate boat operators of which he was one of the few who miraculous survived and that the name "Lazy Lady" was forever burned in his mind. It had been many years ago, but that day and that name was forever burned in the mind of the pirate boat captain.

That golden name often woke him from a nightmare that had him drenched in sweat. He had survived but the hard life of a fisherman had kept him in the pirate trade. Since then, he had moved up in the quality of his attack boat that had three crew members, two gunners and himself. He dropped back from the lead and called the boats with him to cease their pursuit, but they insisted that they had their quarry and were going in for the capture. He watched as one after the other the boats were destroyed and most of the men on those boats killed. It was a repeat of the first time he had interacted with whoever sailed the "Lazy Lady."

He thanked the stars for having dropped back.

His boat and he and his crew were unscathed.

He stopped to pick up the survivors of which there were only three.

When the lead boat began to fire Ian shot the gunner at the machine gun position then he picked up his makeshift bomb and after getting a few swings and judging the distance to the bow he launched the C4 in a high arc. As he watched, it seemed that the pirate boat moved in to catch the bomb on its bow.

The explosion completely tore off the bow, and it looked like the boat was trying to stand on its nose as its speed drove it down into the sea.

The boat directly behind it swung out and began to fire. Mike responded with rapid cover fire while Ian picked up the self-propelled grenade launcher and aimed it for the second boat's bow. The grenade took out the bow and that boat made it halfway into the water before bouncing back out up like a cork, but it came up and was engulfed in flames.

The third boat seemed to follow the same approach and as Mike took the initiative and shot the gunner, Ian fired the second grenade and took out the third boat that repeated what seemed to be a bow first plunge.

The fourth boat stopped and focused on rescuing the men on the first three boats as the Lazy Lady continued sailing on.

Ian noted the helicopter that had been following the action halted its forward progress, hover for a few moments and then turn and fly back toward Mombasa. He wondered if it was an army helicopter and how much of the battle had been recorded.

Andrea had retreated to the kitchen area, but she decided to take up Mike's field camera and crawled out to capture what was taking place. It was hard for her to focus on the action because she kept ducking as if she was the focus of the shooting. She was sure that Mike would have had a steadier hand on the camera.

After the action was over, she came out on deck with Mike's camera and said she had captured the entire engagement and figured she would be able to make it a part of the story that she was planning to call of Rhinos and the Horns of Injustice.

Ian suggested they swing in close to Zanzibar to take them as far off the coast as possible so they would not draw the attention of any other pirates since he was short of ammunition. He had reloaded the two rocket launchers and figured he could handle another round but preferred to savor his win rather than take a chance of a repeat performance and getting someone onboard wounded or worse, killed.

He asked Ted to sail into Dar es Salaam where the team would need to clear Tanzanian customs before catching a flight home.

Ian knew that it would be tricky for him. He would need to use his US passport to be able to show ownership of the Lazy Lady. This was something that he did not want to expose to the team.

He went to the bow for privacy and made a call to his support team. He arranged for a hotel for the team members, located a bank where the millions that he had for each team member could be deposited and for flight reservations and tickets back to the US.

He added the request that all the equipment and suitcases automatically clear the customs inspection at their landing location.

He instructed that the information be sent to Andrea Millar and gave her phone number.

He put in the request for his own and his captains entrance and exit paperwork with the Lazy Lady from Tanzania be immediately issued.

He then returned to the kitchen area and joined the rest of the team.

Somehow their arrival to the Zanzibar port and the pirate attack had become known. A Military boat came out to escort them in. It took them to a peer at the Dar es Salaam port. There were several news crews waiting when they docked, the team was surrounded and bombarded with question on how they had survived the pirate attack.

Ian used this distraction to clear customs and to certify his ownership of the Lazy Lady. He had no plans to disembark but planned to leave as soon as approval to leave was granted.

A call to his support team as they were being escorted in proved to be wise. They had cleared both his arrival and immediate departure after offloading his passengers. They confirmed that they would give Andrea a call as the Lazy Lady left port.

Ted supervised the offloading and once everything was cleared, he cast off.

Andria had been overwhelmed by the onslaught of the news crews all shouting over each other as they asked about the pirate engagement. She turned to see where Matt happened to be and realized that he and Ted had the Lazy Lady heading out of the harbor.

Tears came to her eyes because she figured she would never be able to thank Matt, or whoever he was, for having come to her and the team's rescue. She waved and was pleased to see flashing from what she figured was a mirror.

Her phone buzzed in her pocket, and she read a rather long message explaining that she, her team, their belongings had all cleared customs and that she should proceed to a hotel that had been reserved for her and her team.

She then realized that the four suitcases with five million dollars in each were all lined up with the name of each team member written in black on them and they had the custom clearance papers taped to them.

She had no idea how Matt had pulled that off, but she figured that now it was up to the four of them to get the money put into a bank that she had also been told about.

Later they could move the money to whatever country they planned to live in. She wondered where the money had come from, but she also knew that it was now each team member's money to use as they pleased.

She shook her head as she thought about the fact that they had been kidnapped, had managed to get enough footage to produce a story about the black rhino and were going home with enough money that they could easily retire or do whatever they desired.

It was more than she could process, and she decided to gather the team and get all their things moved to the hotel.

She looked out to where the Lazy Lady was just a dot.

Ian used his binoculars to watch the crowd on the pier. When Andrea turned to look for the Lazy Lady, he used his cell phone to reflect the sun to flash her a goodbye. He wished he could have stayed with the team, but he had accomplished his mission and the problem had been solved.

It was time for him to get back to his Leslie.

Ted figured that the person he knew both as Captain Bitterly and more recently as Mathew Parker were both fictious names. He asked Matt whether he would ever know his real name.

Ian laughed and used the old expression that if he learned his real name he would have to be shot.

He added that instead of worrying about who he was, he should think about how he was going to use the bonus he was getting for doing such a great job as the captain of the Lazy Lady. He was only being rewarded with half of what the camera crew had received because he had only been in on half of the fun that the rest had experienced. But if he accepted the bonus he would have to stop asking about names.

Ted asked what half amounted to and almost fell over when he learned that it was two and a half million dollars. He figured that Matt by any other name would always be Matt to him. The trip across the Atlantic took an entirely new meaning about getting a bonus and how it felt to get a bonus that made him rich.

On the way across the Atlantic, Ian arranged for Ted to take care of the Lazy Lady and keep her active as part of his business.

When they got to Tampa, he thanked Ted for having been a good sailing partner.

They celebrated with a beer and then, he walked down the pier and took a cab to the Airport, took a flight and was soon back to Cincinnati. When he got to the escalator leading to the baggage claim area he looked up and the sunshine of his life was standing at the top smiling down at him.

This was his reward and one that had put the light in his mind on high so that the dark of his mind was manageable and worth more than all the gold in the world.

7 Conclusion

ndria stood staring at the name on the back of the sailing yacht.

She had returned to the states and she and the team had put together another outstanding story that earned all of them the best of the year award from the company that was accompanied with a shopping spree reward. They had also all received a very generous cash bonus.

When asked what she planned to do next she let her boss know that she was leaving to get a PhD in photographic journalism.

Her boss congratulated her and said that the company would grant her a stipend that would cover her tuition to whatever university she selected on the condition that she document her PhD experience and let them have first refusal of her dissertation.

She accepted.

She was accepted to the University of South Florida. It had been one of her top choices because of its location on the Gulf of Mexico coast.

She had become an avid sailor, and on most weekends, she went out sailing with her friends and more recently with a special professor that she was dating.

She had been walking along the boardwalk that made its way along the harbor when in the distance she saw a yacht that seemed familiar, so she had gone down to the dock and walked out on the pier.

Now she was a statue with her feet anchored fast as she stared at the name painted in gold on the aft of the sailing yacht.

It was a very familiar one that was forever emblazoned in her mind.

She was looking at the name, "*Lazy Lady.*"

She was frozen in her spot because she had tears running down her eyes and was afraid to move. Finally, after wiping away her tears, she walk toward the yacht. She wondered if there was anyone on board. As she got nearer, she saw Ted sitting and looking at her.

Ted had been watching the person at the end of the pier.

She looked very familiar, but he was not sure that he was seeing who he thought he was or if his eyes were playing a trick on him.

She finally continued coming toward the Lazy Lady.

He raised his beer that he was sipping and called out to her and suggested she come on board so they could talk about old times.

Andria teared up again.

It was hard to believe that she was once again on the Lazy Lady.

She asked if Ted owned her.

He shook his head and said that the owner was none other than their Matt or whatever his real name might be. He admitted to checking who the person to whom the boat was registered at the marina's main office, and it was registered to a Matthew Bitterly Parker.

He added that the middle name was the one that was used out on the west coast on another of Matt's problem-solving assignments when he had first met him and was the second in command on a twin of the Lazy Lady.

He said that Matt had given him a sizeable bonus for the recent adventure they had on the Lazy Lady on the condition he quit trying to find out his name and with the stipulation that he take care of the Lazy Lady.

He said that he had adhered to both.

He then asked if Andria would care to spend a few hours sailing.

Andria nodded, trying to find her voice to say yes.

Once they were underway, she asked if she could take the wheel and sail her.

As she sailed the Lazy Lady a warm melancholy feeling swept through her. She had relived the adventure in Kenya and the escape that they had made many times.

Now to be sailing the Lazy Lady was like a dream come true.

Later in the afternoon as she was sailing back into the harbor, she asked if she could schedule another outing so that her significant other could experience sailing with her on the Lazy Lady.

She had told that person the entire story of her adventure associated with the filming in Kenya and then the escape on the Lazy Lady.

She was sure that he would love to go out on her.

Ted smiled and said that most weekdays were open, but the Lazy Lady did not get to be lazy on weekends and was booked out for more than three months.

Andria called her significant other and asked if he had any open days. It turned out that he had no classes on Thursdays and used that day to grade papers or prepare for a new lecture topic.

Andria booked the following Thursday.

Ted asked her whether she preferred seafood or red meat for the late lunch meal. He then added that breakfast was made to order and if she wanted a full day out, she would need to be on deck at eight in the morning.

Andria smiled and suggested they stay with seafood and that he should surprise her on what that might be. As she was getting ready to leave, she asked what the cost for such an outing might be.

Ted held up his bottle and said that two cases of beer and two bottles of wine would cover the trip.

Andrea gave him a hug and said she and her significant other would be on time.

Ted watched as Andrea walked away. He was feeling great about her finding the Lazy Lady.

He was just about to call it a day and go home when his phone began to chirp. It was the call of the loon and he had assigned that call to only one person.

Ian had received a brief call from one of his unknown team members informing him that Andria had found the Lazy Lady and asked if there was any concern about the matter. He thanked the caller for the information and said that there was no issue.

He then called Ted to see how sailing with Andria had gone.

Ted answered and was surprised about the question. He asked if he was being watched.

Ian assured him that he was not being watched but that Andria was and would continue to be watched for a few years until whomever the watchers were became satisfied with her safety.

Ted asked whether their Iowa participants on the trip where he had first sailed with him were being watched.

Ian responded that they had been watched for almost a year, but they were never directly in danger like Andrea and her team had been.

Ted then asked if he had been watched.

Ian explained that he had been scrutinized and thoroughly vetted before he had been hired for their first trip together.

Ted laughed and said that so far, he had loved every minute of the experiences he had with Mathew Bitterly Parker and looked forward to another adventure in the future.

Ian chuckled and said that at the right time he would host a reunion of the Kenyan Four and their significant others on the Lazy Lady.

Ted said that he would look forward to the reunion.

Andrea returned to her apartment and spent most of the evening talking about the her sailing the Lazy Lady. She could not get over having gone for a walk and then having spotted a sailing vessel out of all the sail boats anchored in the harbor that turned out to be the Lazy Lady.

That evening she called Mike who now was living in Seatle and let him know about finding the Lazy Lady and taking her out for a several hour sail.

Mike asked if she had run into Matt.

Andrea let him know that Ted did not know where Matt was or how to get in touch with him. She asked if he was open to taking a vacation on the Lazy Lady in the coming summer. By then they might be celebrating her getting her PhD.

Mike agreed that he would love to do that. He figured that the rest of the team would all enjoy such a reunion.

A day later Ian got another call informing him of the planned reunion that would take place in the coming summer. He thanked the caller and said he would wait for them to give him the time, date, and the names of all those that were going to attend.

He said that he wanted to arrange his arrival to the Lazy Lady by helicopter after she passed under the Sunshine Skyway Bridge.

Less than a year later his handlers gave him a call.

Ian was expecting a call focused on a new problem and was pleasantly surprised that the caller gave him the date when his helicopter ride to the Lazy Lady was scheduled. He chuckled and asked what else there was.

His caller told him that the Lazy Lady had been booked for a wedding and a graduation ceremony of an Andria Miller to an Andre Mikles. The date was to be July 15.

Ian asked that a deed for the Lazy Lady be prepared that made Andria the owner with the stipulation that Ted Nickson was to be kept on as the Captain until he decided to retire. He also wanted to have a case of beer delivered to Ted with a message letting him know to expect one additional surprise guest that would arrive in an unusual way.

His caller said, "done" and then hung up.

Ian let Lesley know of the situation and asked if she wanted to go with him.

Lesley said that she would be a fish out of water at the event and that he should plan on attending on his own. She added that for once she would not be home worrying about what danger he was facing.

Ian decided not to share how he planned to board the Lazy Lady.

Andrea worked hard to close her PhD dissertation. The wedding arrangement was the simple part. She did not plan on a wedding dress and chose to have a simple wedding cake. She hired a catering company to prepare for a rather extensive lunch menu, bring it on board and then limit the number of servers to two people.

Her wedding and PhD celebration invitation list was as short as she dared make it. Her parents and Andre's parents were at the top of her list. They were followed by her team members. Andre had his long-time friend be his best man and his brother as a groomsman. She had asked Mary to be her matron of honor.

Ted had been surprised when she asked him to perform the wedding and let her know that he was honored to be asked.

The final list added up to fifteen people and with the two caters there would be seventeen on board.

She cleared the number with Ted to make sure that was acceptable.

Early in the morning on the day of the wedding, Ian left Cincinnati and flew to Tampa. Once there he was met and escorted to where a military helicopter was waiting for him. One of the crew members explained how "T" lift that would lower him to the deck of the yacht worked. They practiced that from twenty feet up before taking him out to the yacht.

The sun was rising when Andria and Andre arrived at the pier where the Lazy Lady was moored. They stood at the head of the pier and greeted their wedding guests and sent them down to where Ted was taking them onboard. The caterers arrived and took the food onboard.

Finally, it was time to depart.

She went to the wheel and stood with Andre at her side as Ted untied the Lazy Lady and jumped on board.

Andrea used the engine to carefully navigate out into the harbor's open area and then raised the main sail. She cautiously sailed out toward the Sunshine Skyway Bridge.

As they were approaching the bridge Ted came to her and asked to take over.

She was surprised but they had been sailing for about an hour and she figured that it was good time to mingle with the rest of the family and friends.

Ted had received a message from Matt that he was making a surprise arrival once the Lazy Lady passed under the bridge. He saw a helicopter hovering on the other side of the bridge and after passing through and sailing for about three football fields he lowered the sail as the chopper came in and hovered about forty feet in the air.

Everyone on board was looking up wondering what was happening.

Andrea started laughing when she saw Matt being lowered from the helicopter.

Ian looked down and waved. He stepped off on the bow and waved up to the pilot as the copter raised the lift, swayed, and then flew away.

Andrea ran up to the bow and gave him a hug, led him back in to the kitchen area and introduced him to Andre, his brother and his parents and then her parents.

She explained that she was alive and here to be wed because of Matt and that his dramatic arrival matched all his other escapades with her and her film crew.

When it came time for the wedding ceremony, Andrea approached Ian and asked if he were a captain and if so, would he take part in the ceremony.

Ian smiled and said that he was not a certified captain but that he was an ordained minister and would be honored to be part of performing her wedding.

Andrea smiled and shook her head and said that seemed such a dichotomy to what he had done in saving her.

Ian nodded and agreed that it even seemed strange to him.

Ted took the sails down and tied the boom off and then stepped in front of the wheel area and ask the bride and groom to step up to his level.

He had Mendelssohn's wedding march playing on the ships sound system as they stepped up to him.

He appreciated the smile on Andrea's face as she stepped up toward him.

Ian was standing at his side and together they performed the wedding.

Andrea was ecstatic as she and Andre exchanged vows and accepted each other's gold wedding rings.

She knew that she had found her soul mate.

And she was especially happy that Matt had arrived in time to perform the wedding.

Ian watched as the two kissed and then stepped down into the kitchen area and received congratulations from everyone on board.

Andrea and Andre cut the small wedding cake and gave each other a bite.

She then led the way to the table where all the gifts were located. She picked up the very official looking certificate. When she realized what it was, she stopped and walked over to Matt and asked if he was serious about giving her the title to the Lazy Lady. She said that having Ted as a perpetual captain was also a great gift.

Ian smiled and said that the Lazy Lady needed to be sailed more often than he had the time to enjoy her. And that he had found the two people that would do just that.

Andrea found it hard to concentrate on the remaining gifts that had been graciously given to her.

The rest of the day was a daze. She kept coming back to the title to the Lazy Lady to make sure it was real.

She realized that she could not read the previous owner's signature and smiled at the fact that even on paper Matt managed to shield his real name.

She picked up the wedding certificate and almost laughed as she took in Matt's long squiggle that was signed below Ted's signature.

Ian enjoyed the rest of the day mingling with the old team and in discussions with both pairs of parents. He felt good about having given the Lazy Lady to Andrea. He planned to buy himself a similar boat if Leslie took to sailing but until then he would enjoy the home where the two of them had spent many wonderful years.

Once they were back to the dock, the partying continued.

Suddenly, Andrea realized that Matt was missing.

She looked up the pier to the very end where she spotted him.

Ian spotted Andrea standing looking his way and with his phone he reflected the sun and sent her a farewell signal. He then turned and walked over to where a taxi was waiting for him.

The End

About the Author

Ronald E. Mueller
remwriter95@gmail.com

Ron grew up in what is now Flint River State Park in Southeast Iowa. The 170-year-old house Ron lived in is built into a hillside. It faces a 125-foot-high cliff towering over the little Flint River. The house and the land talked to him about; the passing of time, the struggle to conquer the land, the struggles people faced and the wonder of nature.

He climbed the cliffs, crawled into the caves, dove from the swimming rock, collected clams from the bottom of the pond, gigged and skinned frogs for their legs. He trapped muskrats for fur, hunted raccoon in the dead of night, and with only a stick hunted rabbits in the dead of winter.

His young life was outdoors, and nature tested him.

He walked to a one room stone schoolhouse uphill both ways. A stern but warm-hearted teacher, Mrs. Henry was instrumental in shaping his character as she shepherded him from the fourth to the eighth grade.

It was a great way to grow up.

Ron graduated from Burlington, High School, went to Vietnam in the Navy. He graduated from The University of South Florida with a master's degree in engineering, worked for thirty eight years for Procter and Gamble, traveled around the world thirty times.

He has remained happily married for more than fifty years. His daughter and his two sons are all successful and his three grandchildren have all graduated.

His wife has humored and supported him as he became a full time professional story teller.

He has come to realize that he is, what is known as, a Cozy writer. Excitement and adventure but little guts and gore. His heroine or hero suffer a little but live happily ever after.

His experiences inter-twined with snippets of fantasy lend themselves to the adventures he leads the reader through.

Books by the Author

<u>Fiction Series</u>
The Alex Evercrest Series
The River Front
The Girl on The Grill
Missing
Maggot
Racist
Votive Candles
Windy City
Country Road
Pool of Blood
Sins of the Daughter
Body Parts
The Skull Collector
The Vanishing
The Shadow Fighter
Moonshine
Grief's Trajectory
The Magic Touch
Northern Lights
Alex Evercrest Heroine
Alex Evercrest Collection Two
New Direction
A Family Affair
Disruption
Aftermath
The St. Lebuinnus Church Murder

A Brian O'Neil Novel
Hawaiian Phoenix
Moon Curser
Death Broker

The Problem Solver Series
Solutions
Drug Lords
Border Crosser
The Problem Solver Collection

<u>The Taelo Series</u>
The Early Years
The Golden Feather
Journey of Discovery
Dangerous Passage
Condor Clan Slingers
Circumvention
The Journey of Sages
Collection
Future Leaders Journey

<u>A Taelo Story:</u>
White Swan and Quiet Pheasant
The Child's Name
Floating Cloud
Quiet Rabbit
Busy Bee
Little Otter & Talking Wren
Broken Spear
Burley Bear & Meadow Flower
Taelo Story Collection

<u>Science Fiction</u>

The Savitar Series:
Journey's End
Savitar
Confluence
Savitar Series Collection

Bram Nielson Series
The Fold
The Message
Fold Wormhole
Negative Fold
Ripples in Time
Bram Nielson Collection

<u>Single Science Fiction Books:</u>
Current Past and Future
The Event
The Door
Viajante 7

Published by: Around the World Publishing LLC.